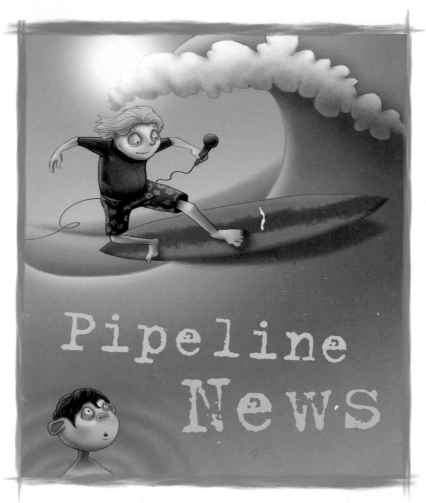

Pipeline News

Lee Aucoin, *Creative Director*
Jamey Acosta, *Senior Editor*
Heidi Fiedler, *Editor*
Produced and designed by
Denise Ryan & Associates
Illustration © Tom Bonson
Rachelle Cracchiolo, *Publisher*

Teacher Created Materials
5301 Oceanus Drive
Huntington Beach, CA 92649-1030
http://www.tcmpub.com
Paperback: ISBN 978-1-4333-5635-3
Library Binding ISBN: 978-1-4807-1734-3
© 2014 Teacher Created Materials

Written by
Bill Condon

Illustrated by
Tom Bonson

Contents

Pipeline News

LALI: Wakey, wakey, people! It's six A.M., and you're listening to Lali on Hawaii's PNN, the Pipeline News Network!

Now, it's time for the show you've all been waiting for—*Pipeline News!* Let's go live to Brad. Tell us what's happening on the Big Island, Brad.

Big
Island

BRAD: Brad here, reporting from the PNN chopper! Right now, I'm flying low over the Big Island. It's beautiful!

I can see the golden beaches and the waving palm trees. Now, as I get even closer, I can see those enormous coconuts. They're so tempting, and I'm so thirsty.

Wait one second, listeners. I'm putting the chopper on autopilot while I reach out to grab a coconut. Whoa! That wasn't the autopilot button— it was the ejector seat! Yee-haw! This is one cool ride! I can see for miles!

Hey, there's a school of dolphins! And it seems like some careless guy has lost his chopper. Whoops, that's mine.

But I haven't got time to worry about that because now I'm about to splash down in three... two...one! Here we go!

Man, oh man, it's a fine day for surfing! The water is perfect! There are surfers all around, and they are flying across the waves!

But wait, that's weird. They're all heading back to the beach. Now, they're sounding an alarm. And I see teeth—a lot of teeth.

Oh, my! That wasn't a school of dolphins. It was a shiver of sharks!

This is Brad, signing off from the Big Island.

LALI: Thanks for that update, Brad. Let's go now to Rad...

Kauai

RAD: I'm surfing off the island of Kauai. And I'm about to do an aerial. I'm going to launch my board from the top of a wave. It's very tricky, surfers, so leave it to an expert, like me.

Here I go! Well…actually, I couldn't do it. But I did perform another amazing trick called a *wipeout*.

LALI: Well done, Rad. What's it like out there today?

RAD: It's wet, Lali. Very wet. There's water everywhere.

LALI: Do you have any other details?

RAD: Sure do. I've got air temperature, water temperature, high tide, low tide, swell trackers, and storm warnings. I've got traffic reports, volcano reports, water quality, and air quality.

And, for the first ten surfers to come up to me and say, "I love Pipeline News!" I've got a tube of sunscreen and a free balloon!

I've got it all!

LALI: Fantastic!

13

RAD: The only thing I don't have is my board shorts. I left home in such a hurry this morning that I forgot all about them. It's a good thing this is radio and no one can see me!

LALI: Um, Rad, is there a plane circling above you?

RAD: As a matter of fact, there is.

LALI: Does it have TV News on it?

RAD: Yes...I think it does.

LALI: Congratulations, Rad. You're a TV star!

RAD: Aaaaaaaggghhh! This is Rad, signing off from Kauai!

15

Maui

LALI: Now, we go to Tad.

TAD: Welcome to wonderful Maui!
There's always something wild
going on down here.

17

Today, we had a sandcastle
competition. And we also
staged the famous Maui
Elephant Run.

The sandcastles were incredible!
So intricate! So clever! And
so flattened! Maybe next year
they should have the elephant
run on a different day than the
sandcastle competition.

Meanwhile, out in the surf, the
waves are as high as skyscrapers,
and there's a cyclone heading
this way. There's also a chance
of an underwater volcanic
eruption and possibly a tsunami.
But otherwise, conditions are
ideal for surfing!

Even the jellyfish are enjoying
it. As an added bonus, there is a
school of very unusual fish that
are playfully nibbling at my toes.

And now, adding to the excitement, a humpback whale has surfaced beside me. Maui is one of the best places in the world for whale watching, but this whale seems to be watching me! I think it wants to play, so I'm going to go a little closer... closer...just a little closer.

Wow! I've stumbled into an underwater cave. How lucky is that? It's so dark in here, and it smells kind of fishy. I wonder where that whale went—oops!

LALI: Are you okay, Tad? Tad? Seems like we've lost contact with Tad.

We'll go now to Jad.

Oahu

JAD: Yes, Jad here. There are several surfers out here with me, waiting to catch the next set of waves.

23

You might wonder what surfers do while they're waiting for a wave. Well, I'll tell you. Some are reading books. One is eating his breakfast (spaghetti on toast). One is talking on his cell phone, and another is strumming a guitar.

There's one crazy dude doing his ironing! He's probably an iron man. There are a few practicing surfing tricks. One guy is hanging five. One is hanging ten, and one is just hanging on—oh, that's me.

Here comes a wave! Up we go, riding the crest! And down we go! Gnarly, dudes!

The tube is throwing us around like corks! Just one fearless surfer is staying on his board!

It's me! Look at me go! No one has ever done cutbacks and aerials better than this! I'm going to be a legend. I'm...uh...oh, I'm in big trouble!

This is terrible! Awful! My mother has paddled out, and she isn't happy. Sorry, Lali, I have to go home—right now. I forgot to clean my room this morning.

LALI: Okay, Jad, make sure you do a good job.

Well, surfers, now you've got all the information you need to hit the boards and power through those waves! That brings us to the conclusion of *Pipeline News*. Thanks for listening, and happy surfing!

LALI: *Pipeline News* was brought to you by the enchanted Hawaiian Islands. The Hawaiian Islands are located in the Pacific Ocean. Together, they form the state of Hawaii, the fiftieth state to join the United States of America. Hawaii is made up of six main islands and many smaller islands and reefs. You can take surfing lessons on almost every island.

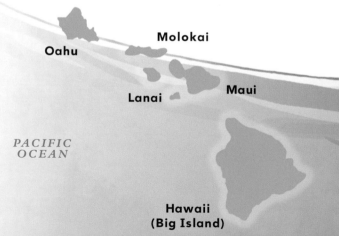

Kauai

Molokai

Oahu

Lanai

Maui

PACIFIC OCEAN

Hawaii
(Big Island)

And here's another word from our sponsors….

Get your feet wet and ride your first wave in Waikiki Beach. Known for its gentle, rolling waves, this beach is perfect for beginners and beyond. Grab a board and catch a wave today!

The Pipeline News Team

Tad

Jad

30

Brad

Rad

They never let you down...
well, at least they're fun to
listen to.

31

Bill Condon lives in the seaside town of Woonona, Australia. When not writing, Bill plays tennis, snooker, and Scrabble but hardly ever at the same time. Bill has won many awards for his writing, including the Prime Minister's Literary Award in 2010. Bill wrote *The Human Calculator*, *How to Survive in the Jungle by the Person Who Knows*, and *Race to the Moon* for Read! Explore! Imagine! Fiction Readers.

Tom Bonson lives in Bristol, England. He loves creating quirky characters that everyone can enjoy. Tom illustrated *Where Did the Dinosaurs Go?* and *Your Guide to Superheroes* for Read! Explore! Imagine! Fiction Readers.